Into the painting . . .

"What do you think?" Steve asked Uncle Fong. When he sat back, the sunlight from the window flooded the room. His grandfather and uncle crowded around.

"But what will you do when we want to go to bed?" Uncle Fong asked.

Quickly Steve painted a shutter. "We'll cover up the window with this."

"It looks just like home," Uncle Fong murmured as he gazed at the village.

Grandfather squinted at the window. "The trees look like they're swaying in a breeze," he said. "That's very artful of you, Steve."

Uncle Fong rested against the window as he sniffed the air. "And the peaches are just ripening. You got the season just right, boy."

As Uncle Fong bent to touch a peach, he leaned too far. With a cry, he toppled straight into the painting.

ALSO BY LAURENCE YEP

The Dragon Prince
Dream Soul
The Imp That Ate My Homework
The Rainbow People
The Star Fisher
Sweetwater
Tongues of Jade

GOLDEN MOUNTAIN CHRONICLES

The Serpent's Children
Mountain Light
Dragon's Gate
A Newbery Honor Book
The Traitor
Dragonwings
A Newbery Honor Book
The Red Warrior
Coming Soon
Child of the Owl
Sea Glass
Thief of Hearts

CHINATOWN MYSTERIES

The Case of the Goblin Pearls
Chinatown Mystery #1
The Case of the Lion Dance
Chinatown Mystery #2
The Case of the Firecrackers
Chinatown Mystery #3

DRAGON OF THE LOST SEA FANTASIES

Dragon of the Lost Sea
Dragon Steel
Dragon Cauldron
Dragon War

EDITED BY LAURENCE YEP

American Dragons
Twenty-Five Asian American Voices

LAURENCE YEP

THE MAGIC PAINTBRUSH

DRAWINGS BY SULING WANG

HarperTrophy®
An Imprint of HarperCollinsPublishers

To Felicia, who has a magical brush of her own
—L.Y.

Harper Trophy® is a registered trademark of HarperCollins Publishers Inc.

The Magic Paintbrush
Text copyright © 2000 by Laurence Yep
Illustrations copyright © 2000 by Suling Wang

Library of Congress Cataloging-in-Publication Data
Yep, Laurence.
  The magic paintbrush / by Laurence Yep ; drawings by Suling Wang.
    p.   cm.
  Summary: A magic paintbrush transports Steve and his elderly caretakers from their drab apartment in Chinatown to a world of adventures.
  ISBN 0-06-028199-5. — ISBN 0-06-028200-2 (lib. bdg.)
  ISBN 0-06-440852-3 (pbk.)
  1. Chinese Americans—Juvenile fiction. [1. Chinese Americans—Fiction. 2. Grandfathers—Fiction. 3. Old age—Fiction. 4. Magic—Fiction. 5. Wishes—Fiction. 6. Orphans—Fiction. 7. Chinatown (San Francisco, Calif.)—Fiction.] I. Wang, Suling, ill. II. Title.
PZ7.Y44Mag 2000   99-34959
[Fic]—dc21   CIP

Typography by Carla Weise
15 16 17 CG/OPM 20 19 18 17 16
❖
First Harper Trophy edition, 2003

Visit us on the World Wide Web!
www.harperchildrens.com

CONTENTS

Failure

Steve sat in the school yard long after school was over. He was really scared. What would his grandfather say when Steve went home? He preferred shivering outside to facing his grandfather.

All around the school yard the buildings of Chinatown crowded shoulder to shoulder. Everything here seemed so strange. It was one big nightmare.

Resting his head on his knees, he closed his eyes. Maybe when he opened them, he'd be back home where there were regular houses and real lawns. And his mother and father would be waiting in the doorway.

He tried to remember what they looked like, but all he could see were flames. He screwed his eyebrows together as he fought to recall them. No matter how hard he struggled, they were always hidden by fire.

He was all alone now—except for his grandfather. And that was the same thing as being alone.

Grandfather was mean. Steve knew his grandfather didn't want him. After the fire he had to go live in Chinatown. Grandfather had told Steve he could bring only one box with him to Chinatown. How do you put your whole life into just one box? Not that he had much left after the fire. He had lost everything . . . his parents, his toys, his books, his clothes.

And everything Steve did just made his grandfather meaner. He never spoke to Steve except to scold him. And now Steve was sure his grandfather was going to blow his top.

Steve had always tried to get good grades when his parents were alive, especially in art, his favorite class. His parents had hung his best paintings in their offices so their coworkers could admire them. The rest of their house had been decorated with them.

All that was gone in one terrible, fiery night.

Now, because his grandfather was poor, there was never money for watercolors or paper. Steve had to make everything last: his clothes, his paper, his pens, and especially his paints and paintbrush.

Back at home, he would have enjoyed today's assignment. He would have painted a great portrait of the new president, Kennedy.

However, today at school the brush had worn out.

The tired hairs had refused to keep their point and had split into three parts.

His third-grade teacher had criticized his painting. "You're straining my eyes. I feel like I'm seeing triple. How many times have I reminded you to get a new brush?"

"I'm sorry," Steve said. He was too ashamed to tell her that he could not afford a new one.

"You should have obeyed me. Maybe this will teach you," she had said, and she wrote a big "F" on his picture.

The rest of the day Steve was in a daze. He had never gotten an F before, and he had never thought he would get it in his best subject.

He opened his eyes now. He was still caught in the nightmare, and it was getting worse. The Chinatown shadows were growing longer. All around him the doorways started to look like mouths. They stretched wide to swallow him.

Finally he got more scared of the Chinatown streets than of his grandfather. Slowly he walked through the narrow alleys until he reached his grandfather's apartment building. Steve couldn't think of the ugly building as his home.

The tenement house was all of dark-red brick. Dirt made the bricks look even darker. It had a narrow front that rose for three stories.

As Steve mounted the steps, he heard shouting from the back. Everyone in the tenement shared the kitchen, with its sink and stove. The tenants were supposed to take turns, but there were always fights.

"Hey," Mrs. Lee yelled, "it's time to get out of here."

"I can't help it," Mrs. Chin shouted back. "The people ahead of me took longer."

"And afterward clean up the stove and the sink for the next person," Mrs. Lee snapped.

Their angry voices chased him up the dim stairs. Their words nipped at his ears. The Chins and the Lees always seemed to be fighting over something.

He stopped when he reached his floor. The landlord, Mr. Pang, never replaced the ceiling lights. The hallway stretched on like a black tunnel. It looked like raw, dark dough that someone was pulling longer and longer.

There was just one toilet on each floor of the tenement. It was always leaking. Steve could hear it dripping now. And yet Mr. Pang was always raising the rent. Whenever anyone complained, Mr. Pang told them to go back to China if they didn't like his building.

Steve found his way by smell: past Mrs. Soo, who was burning incense in her room. He found his way by ear: past Mr. Jow and his bad, bloody cough. He found his way by touch: past the old, moldy mattress leaning against the wall.

Groping, he found the door to the room he shared with his grandfather and Uncle Fong. Taking a deep breath, he twisted the doorknob and stepped inside.

The bare bulb dangling from the ceiling cast a harsh light over the tiny, cramped room. The paint on the old walls was peeling or stained orange and brown where the rain had leaked or pipes had burst. It was tiny compared to his old bedroom. This room was barely ten by ten feet. A small table stood near the doorway as he entered. On the table were their hot plate, glasses, dishes, and chopsticks. None of the dishes matched. Most of them came from restaurants where Grandfather had washed dishes.

Against one wall was the bed that belonged to Uncle Fong. On the opposite wall was Steve and Grandfather's bed. The room was a crazy quilt of colors. Every inch was crammed with boxes and shopping bags full of Grandfather's and Uncle Fong's stuff. The room was so packed, there was barely enough room for Steve's things.

His grandfather looked at him angrily.

"Where have you been?" Grandfather frowned. "We've waited to have dinner with you."

That made Steve feel more guilty. He knew that Grandfather and Uncle Fong had been working since dawn that morning.

Uncle Fong was sitting on his bed, soaking his feet in a basin of water. "Shame on you," he scolded. "Eight-year-old boys shouldn't be out this late on their own."

Uncle Fong was not a blood relation. He came from Dragon Back, a village in China next to Grandfather's, and they had been friends since they were boys. After Grandmother had died, they had become roommates. They had lived together for a long time now.

Grandfather glared at Steve. "Native-born have no brains."

"Your grandfather was worried sick," Uncle Fong said. "Don't you realize how hard it is for a man your grandfather's age to have to raise a boy?"

"You were worried about me?" Steve asked, surprised. He had thought his grandfather would be glad if he left.

"Of course," his grandfather snapped. Annoyed, he plugged in the hot plate and turned it on.

Mr. Pang did not allow hot plates. However, it was easier to cook meals in their room than in the kitchen. Soon Steve could smell the sausages and vegetables heating up on top of the rice in the pot.

His stomach started to growl. It had been hours since lunchtime.

"Where were you, you bad boy?" Uncle Fong demanded.

How could he tell Grandfather and Uncle Fong about what had happened at school? Too miserable to speak, Steve sat upon the bed.

Grandfather came over and felt his forehead. "What's wrong, boy? Are you sick?"

Steve knew he could not put it off any longer, so he reached into his backpack and took out his picture. "I tried my best, but the teacher gave me an F."

He tensed, getting ready for the scolding. Would his grandfather get so mad, he'd throw Steve out?

Then what would Steve do?

Grandfather's Suitcase

G randfather studied the picture for a while. He squinted at it up close and then held it far away. Finally he harrumphed. "Actually, I think it's rather clever. How did you copy everything three times the same way? It's very, very artful. I would have given you an A."

Uncle Fong came over on his wet feet to look at it himself. "Fool, he didn't do that deliberately. There's something wrong with his brush."

"Let me see your paintbrush," Grandfather said, holding out his hand.

Steve got out his precious watercolors and opened the lid. "I've tried to make it last." He held up the tired brush.

"It's got less hair than Fong." Grandfather rubbed

the top of Uncle Fong's bald head.

Uncle Fong straightened up. "Those cheap brushes never last long. You've got to buy him a new one."

Grandfather patted his pants pockets, but they were empty. "I don't get paid until Friday."

Uncle Fong went back to his bed and set his feet in the basin. "I'm broke too," he said.

"Then it's more Fs until next week." Steve sniffed. Tears started to roll down his cheeks.

His grandfather hesitated and then patted him clumsily on the shoulder. "Don't cry. It's not your fault. It's not anyone's fault."

That only made Steve feel worse, and he cried even harder.

"Well, well," his grandfather said, scratching his cheek and studying him. Suddenly he squatted down. When Steve had tried that position once, he had had to give up. His hip and leg joints had ached too much.

Reaching beneath the bed, Grandfather dragged out an old brown suitcase. "I got all this old junk I should have thrown away a long time ago."

Curious, Steve wiped his eyes on his sleeve. "Are there any pictures of my parents in there?" He had lost all his photographs in the fire.

Grandfather became solemn. His eyes narrowed and his lips pressed together tightly. He looked as if Steve had kicked him. That always happened whenever Steve mentioned his parents. His grandfather must hate Steve's parents as much as he hated Steve.

"What's past is past," Grandfather scolded. "You can't spend the rest of your life missing someone or something. Life is hard, so you have to be hard too. You've got a lot to learn about being a Chinatowner. Chinatowners have to grow up fast. Uncle Fong did. I did. Now it's your turn."

Steve had never felt more lonely. Grandfather could be really strange. Steve would never understand him.

"I'm sorry," Steve said quickly, before Grandfather could lose his temper again.

Grandfather looked back at the suitcase. "Anyway, this junk is even older than your father."

The brass locks clicked up, and Grandfather lifted the top. The smell of sandalwood filled the room. It was pungent but pleasant. Steve leaned to look over Grandfather's shoulder. There were many objects inside. He pointed toward a metal tonguelike object. "What's that, Grandfather?"

"A shoehorn." Grandfather picked it up and placed it near his heel. "It helps you put on your shoes." He held it up so Steve could read what was printed on the shoehorn. "It's from the old Roos Brothers Department Store." He put the shoehorn back into the suitcase. "I got my first pair of American shoes there. I thought they were so fancy. And then afterward I had my first ice cream. It was at Blum's."

"I don't suppose you have a souvenir from that?"

Uncle Fong asked, and smacked his lips. "It looks like you've got everything else in there."

"Fifty years of junk," Grandfather agreed.

His words made it sound as if he didn't care, but he was looking inside the suitcase wistfully. Steve would have liked to ask Grandfather more questions. Were there reminders of Grandmother in there? But he was too scared to ask.

All the attention had made his grandfather cranky. Shifting the suitcase, he shielded the contents with his body. "It's all from places no one cares about anymore," he mumbled. "When I got some time, I'm going to throw it all out."

Steve had felt terrible when he had lost everything in the fire. "No, don't do that. All those things must have special memories, or you wouldn't have kept them."

"Don't encourage him. He's a regular pack rat," Uncle Fong said.

"At least I've got memories. What have you got?" Grandfather asked Uncle Fong.

Now that water had softened his corns and calluses, Uncle Fong began to trim them. "Nothing. I should have stayed in Dragon Back. I can't even stay warm here. No heat in the meat-packing place and no heat here. But it was always hot back home."

"I wish you'd stop talking about China all the time," Grandfather grumbled. "I'd settle for a room with a window. It'd be nice to see a little blue sky once in a while. All I see the whole day is dirty plates. Sometimes what I see on them makes my stomach get sick. Then I don't want to eat."

"At least you get variety. When you cut chickens all day, all you see is one chicken rump after another." Uncle Fong made a face. "I see chicken rumps even in my dreams now."

Grandfather sighed to Steve. "Can you believe anyone trusts that sour old man with a knife?"

Steve did not answer. He didn't want the teasing to escalate into another one of their arguments. They could be like two boys in a school yard. The playful insults could go on until one of them went over a line. Then words could turn to punches.

As Grandfather continued to sift through the contents of the suitcase, Steve heard mysterious clinkings and clackings. They sounded like music, and Grandfather looked as if he were far away. Steve wondered what Grandfather was remembering.

"Ah," Grandfather finally said when he found what he wanted. "Here. You can use this, Steve."

When he turned around, Grandfather had a brush in his hands.

The Magic Paintbrush

The paintbrush was a work of art in itself. Its bamboo stem had been intricately carved. Though Steve studied the carvings, he could not make them out. They were too old and worn.

And yet the brush itself seemed new. Its blue hairs looked pure and crisp. They tapered to a sharp point.

Grandfather twirled the stem between his fingers. "My grandfather made this for me before I came here. He said the hairs came from a unicorn's tail. Or was it a dragon's beard? Here, boy. Take the brush."

Though Steve longed to touch it, he kept his hands at his sides. "I couldn't use this. It's too special."

"Go on, boy," Uncle Fong urged. "That was only a story his grandfather told him. Dragons and unicorns. Bah! I bet there was some poor horse back in China that felt a draft on its south end."

"This looks new," Steve said. "Didn't you ever use it?"

"I was supposed to continue my art lessons here, but I was always too busy working." Grandfather thrust the brush at Steve. "Go on. It's just gathering dust."

"Thank you." Breathlessly, Steve took the paintbrush. He remembered to add, "Granddad."

"Forget it," his grandfather said, but he sounded pleased.

The bamboo stem felt warm in Steve's fingers. It began to tingle. The carvings even seemed to wriggle, tickling his fingers. The paintbrush begged to be used. He couldn't wait any longer. "Can I try it out?"

"So you like that old thing?" his grandfather asked shyly.

"Eat your dinner first," Uncle Fong scolded.

Steve's stomach was growling again, but he wanted to paint even more. "I'm not hungry," he fibbed.

Grandfather studied him thoughtfully. "You love to paint, don't you?"

Steve caressed the stem. "It's my favorite subject in school."

Grandfather smiled. "I used to be just like you. Well, go on. We'll get things ready."

"You spoil him," Uncle Fong grumbled.

"I don't want him turning out all sour like you," Grandfather teased.

"You're a fine one to talk. You'd outsour a lemon,"

16

Uncle Fong said. He watched Steve sit eagerly on the floor. Scratching his nose, Uncle Fong pulled out a pile of paper from under his bed. "I went through the trash can in the office. I figure you can use the backs." He tried to look like he didn't care. "Or you can just toss the paper in the trash."

"Thank you, Uncle Fong," Steve said. Finding paper was always a problem. Fortunately there was an office at the meat plant. "Can I throw away your basin of water?"

"If you like," Uncle Fong said, trying hard not to smile.

Steve went to the bathroom and emptied the basin into the sink. After he had cleaned it out, he put in some fresh water and returned to the room. He had left the door open so that he could find his way back in the dark hallway.

As Steve returned, he could hear Grandfather and Uncle Fong talking.

"I want a steak tonight," Uncle Fong demanded. Every night he asked for something expensive. It was his idea of a joke.

"Beef costs too much," Grandfather snapped. Then his face took on a mischievous look. "However," he added, "tonight we have some for you."

"Really?" Uncle Fong said, surprised.

"Of course we do," Grandfather said. "Would I lie?" He did not give Uncle Fong a chance to reply.

"You remember Ah Deer, the butcher? He owed me money from a bet. So he paid me off. I . . . uh . . . snuck it into the pot when you weren't looking. The beef is almost as tender as Dragon Back beef."

"That steak would have to be very tender then. Is it?" Uncle Fong asked Grandfather.

As soon as Steve appeared in the doorway, Grandfather crooked a finger at him. When Steve leaned over, Grandfather whispered, "Let's grant Uncle's wish. Can you paint him a steak?"

Since Uncle Fong had given him the paper, Steve didn't know if he should help with the prank. "I don't know . . ." he said uncertainly.

Grandfather just winked. "Come on, boy. Be a sport."

Grandfather had never asked him to share anything, even a joke. So Steve got his paints and selected a sheet of white paper. On the front was a list of prices, but the back was pure white. When Steve picked up the brush, he felt the tingle again.

Steve painted a steak bone. The brush tip darted hungrily at the paper like a snake. He put in the red meat and the white veins and even remembered the government seal of approval.

Just as he finished, the lid began to bounce up and down on the pot.

"Dinner's ready," Grandfather announced, and lifted the lid.

Uncle Fong got up from his bed and went over to the pot. "I thought you said there was beef," he complained.

"No, no, there's a steak all for you." Grandfather waved at Steve to give the painting to Uncle Fong.

When Steve grasped the painting, it tingled against his fingertips. He felt as if he had rubbed his shoes fast over a carpet. And the tingling spread through his whole hand.

Dangling from his hand was a big, juicy, red steak. "What's going on?" he asked, scared.

Grandfather and Uncle Fong had their backs to him. When he turned around, Grandfather gave a jump. "Where did that come from?"

"It just appeared," Steve said as he turned the steak this way and that. He studied it from several angles. "I . . . I just painted it," Steve said.

Still holding the lid, Grandfather inspected it.

Uncle Fong leaned over and gave it a sniff. "It smells like beef."

Grandfather poked it with a finger. "It feels like beef."

Uncle Fong folded his arms. "Ha, ha. Very funny, Steve. You're an even worse prankster than your grandfather. You can't fool me. That steak came from Ah Deer."

"No. I was kidding about Ah Deer. The brush really is magic," Grandfather said, staring at it.

Uncle Fong got a frying pan from beneath the table. "Well, magic or not, we're going to eat it." He began to rummage around. "Let's see. Where's the knife?"

Steve picked up the brush. It felt warm, as if it were alive. "Maybe I can make one. What kind would you like?"

Uncle Fong still thought Steve was playing a joke. "I don't care as long as it has an edge."

Quickly, Steve cleaned his brush. Selecting another piece of paper, he began to paint a cleaver with a sharp edge. Once again the brush almost seemed to pull his fingers along. When he was finished, he put the brush down. Then he picked up the paper.

He felt a tingle pass through the paper and into his hand. Carefully he laid the picture down on his bed. Suddenly a cleaver appeared on top of the covers.

Uncle Fong set the pan down with a clunk. "Huh! The brush really is magic."

Heart's Desire

"W e're rich! We're rich! We're rich!" Uncle Fong shouted, and did a little dance. He stopped when the neighbors beneath them pounded on the ceiling.

Uncle Fong was too happy to stop completely. "We're rich, we're rich," he whispered back to the neighbors.

Sitting back down on his bed, he said in an even lower voice, "Now Steve can paint money whenever we need it."

Grandfather poked him in the chest. "Fool! Everyone in Chinatown knows we're poor. They'll think we stole it from someone."

"Steve could demonstrate for them," Uncle Fong said. "Then he can paint me a big, fancy car." He raised his hands and pretended to turn a big steering wheel.

Grandfather lowered Uncle Fong's arms. "Someone will steal the brush then," Grandfather said. "If people knew our secret, they would want things too. They could gang up on us."

Uncle Fong looked very frustrated. He began to slice the beef quickly. "If you can't use it, what good is magic then?"

Grandfather rubbed his chin. "We can use the brush. We just have to be careful. We must continue to dress the same. We must act the same. We must follow the same routine."

Uncle Fong groaned. "You mean go to work?"

"And school," Grandfather said, glancing at Steve.

"And tell our secret to no one." Uncle Fong started to fry the beef with quick flicks of his wooden chopsticks. "Well, at least we can feast every night."

"We don't know how much magic is in the brush," Grandfather said. "Magic isn't like ink. It doesn't work like a disposable pen." He spread his arms. "If we don't use it correctly, we're out of luck and out of magic. We need to use the paintbrush carefully."

Uncle Fong looked toward Heaven. "Isn't that just my luck? Now I can't even count on eating well."

Grandfather crossed his legs. "What would you do if you were rich?"

Uncle Fong sulked. "I told you. I'd drive a big car."

"That's a toy." Grandfather clasped his hands over his knees. "You'd get bored with it soon. And wait till you try to find a parking space."

"Chinatown is jammed with cars and trucks day and night," Uncle Fong admitted.

Grandfather cleared his throat. "In other words, what would make you happy?"

"Well, I . . ." Uncle Fong said, and then scratched his head. "You know, I'm not sure. I never thought about that part."

Grandfather wagged one leg up and down. "Just so. None of us have. We don't want money. We want what money can buy. We want our hearts' desire, as the poets say."

Steve looked at his grandfather, impressed. He hadn't thought Grandfather was such a wise man.

Grandfather awkwardly patted Steve on the back. "Steve can give us our dreams."

Uncle Fong shook his head. "I gave up dreaming a long time ago."

"Then start again, old man," Grandfather said.

The beef sizzled in the pan. "In the meantime, can we eat?" Steve asked. He had not tasted beef in a long time.

"This boy is as smart as his grandfather. The beef's done." Uncle Fong laughed and ladled the beef into a dish.

All through dinner everyone kept looking at the magic brush. Finally Uncle Fong set down his bowl and patted his stomach. "What a feast."

"Almost as good as Dragon Back beef?" Grandfather asked.

Uncle Fong was feeling good. For once something had equaled his old home. "Almost."

When they had cleaned up everything, they sat down on their beds. As Steve picked up the brush again in his right hand, he felt it tremble in his fingers. "So what do I paint next?"

"I would like a peach from home." Uncle Fong closed his eyes. "One with a lovely scent that fills the room. And when you bite into it, the juice runs into your mouth. And it's as sweet as summer. And the scent is like perfume."

"That's a tall order," Grandfather said, glancing uncertainly at Steve.

Uncle Fong folded his arms. "That's what I want."

"And anyway, who said you could go first?" Grandfather demanded.

Steve thought he saw a way to please both old men. In his hand he felt the brush twitching eagerly. He had to use two hands to keep it still. "Do you still want a window, Grandfather?"

"Yes," Grandfather said.

"And just when I was starting to think you were smart," Uncle Fong said in disgust. "A window on any of our walls would just look at another brick wall."

Steve turned on his bed and rose to his knees. "No. I think I know what to do."

On the bare wall above his and Grandfather's bed he painted a window that looked just like a Chinese window. He had seen one in an antique store. The window frame was of carved wood that had been painted red. It was covered with flowers and dragons and unicorns.

Steve's window turned out perfectly. Feeling much more confident now, he turned to Uncle Fong. "What was your home like?"

Uncle Fong licked his lips. "Well, Dragon Back village sat on the side of a valley. There were pine trees along the ridge. And there were rice fields on the valley floor. They looked just like emerald patches." As he talked, the frown lines left the corners of his mouth. He looked younger as he remembered his hometown. "And the orchards surrounded the village. You could always find my family's pet duck there. It was always hunting for food."

As Uncle Fong stood over his shoulder, Steve began to paint the village between the window frames. He hardly needed Uncle Fong's coaching. The brush already seemed to know exactly what to paint. The ridge rising from the valley was shaped like a dragon. The green-tiled roofs were like scales. The pine trees stood up like spikes from the dragon's spine. The fields on the valley floor looked like stained glass.

Finally Steve painted an orchard of peach trees just for Uncle Fong. The peaches shimmered like pale stars. As a last touch he added a duck under the trees.

"What do you think?" Steve asked Uncle Fong. When he sat back, the sunlight from the window flooded the room. His grandfather and uncle crowded around.

"Does it still feel like a tomb in here now?" Steve asked Grandfather timidly.

He was pleased when Grandfather shook his head. "Blue sky—just like I always wanted."

"But what will you do when we want to go to bed?" Uncle Fong asked.

Quickly Steve painted a shutter. "We'll cover up the window with this."

"It looks just like home," Uncle Fong murmured as he gazed at the village.

Grandfather squinted at the window. "The trees look like they're swaying in a breeze," he said. "That's very artful of you, Steve."

Uncle Fong rested against the window as he sniffed the air. "And the peaches are just ripening. You got the season just right, boy."

As Uncle Fong bent to touch a peach, he leaned too far. With a cry, he toppled straight into the painting.

Home Cooking

"Are you all right?" Steve called.

A tiny Uncle Fong waved to them from inside the picture. "I'm fine. Come on. Join me," he shouted. He sounded far away.

"You old fool! Come back here," Grandfather called urgently.

Uncle Fong made a face at Grandfather. "I'll race you. Just like the old days."

"I don't have time for your silly games," Grandfather snapped. "What about your corns and calluses?"

"Coward!" Uncle Fong forgot all about his aching feet. He began to run. He looked as excited as a small boy.

When he disappeared among the trees, Grandfather sighed. "We'd better follow him. He might get into trouble. Bring that paintbrush with you, boy." Gingerly,

Grandfather stepped into the window. When he saw it was safe, he let Steve step through the painting.

Together they entered the orchard. Overhead the peaches hung among the leafy green branches. The fruity perfume surrounded them like a cloud.

They heard a rattling sound ahead of them. When they stepped out of the cover of the trees, they saw an odd wooden machine. "What is that?" Steve asked.

"It's a water chain," Grandfather said. "It carries water from the river."

The water chain was a long wooden trough. It led from the river up the slope. Inside the trough was a series of wooden paddles.

Uncle Fong held on to a wooden stick. His feet moved a wheel of wooden pedals. "Come on. I bet I can bring more water up than you."

Grandfather shook his head. "That's how you always tried to trick me into doing that chore."

Uncle Fong tossed his head back and laughed. "It never worked, though." Then he looked at Steve. "When I was your age, boy, I always hated this job. I didn't know how good I had it. This is fun next to working at the meat packer's."

As his feet turned the wheel, the chain moved. Water splashed from the upper end of the trough into a ditch. The ditch fed water into the orchard.

"Ow," said Grandfather. The next moment Steve felt something nip his ankle. He looked at his feet. There squatted a very annoyed and self-important duck.

"I thought it was a pet?" Steve said as he rubbed his leg.

"To be more exact, it was his sister's pet, and she encouraged it to bite boys." Grandfather darted away from the snapping beak.

Uncle Fong jumped down from the pedals. "Go on. Shoo, Coconut." He waved his hands to make it go away.

When the duck charged him, he got down on all fours and began to growl. The duck halted but began to quack angrily. When Uncle Fong barked back, the duck waddled off. Uncle Fong chased it to the edge of the orchard. Then he stood up.

"Try a peach, Steve," Uncle Fong said. He plucked three from the nearest branch.

The sweetness soaked into Steve's tongue when he bit into his.

Uncle Fong smacked his lips. "It's just as good as I remembered."

"It's good enough for a banquet in Heaven," Grandfather decided.

They heard a little girl singing. She was a little off-key. Soon she danced into view. In her hand she had a long, red ribbon, which she twirled overhead in circles and spirals.

"That's my big sister, Kitten," Uncle Fong said softly to Steve. "She died many years ago."

"She looks like you," Steve whispered back.

Uncle Fong got annoyed. "No, she's the ugly one. I'm the handsome one," he protested.

"What's the difference? You haven't seen her in years," Grandfather said.

Uncle Fong stared at his sister while she danced. Slowly his mouth worked up into a smile. "Well anyway, Kitten may not have been better-looking than me, but she was always more graceful."

When the ribbon snagged in a tree's branches, Uncle Fong went over to her. "Let me help you, big sister."

When she saw him, her eyes got really big. "Who are you?! Don't you dare steal our fruit!" She began shouting. "Help! Thieves! Rascals!"

Uncle Fong held out his hands to her. "Don't you know me? I've come a long way to see you."

When she frowned, she looked exactly like Uncle Fong. "Well, watch this," Kitten said, and grabbed Uncle Fong's thumb. Then she bit it. Hard.

"Ow!" Uncle Fong said. He wrung his hurt hand in the air.

"That's where her duck gets its personality from." Grandfather laughed.

Uncle Fong clenched his good hand into a fist. "She always had a temper," he explained to Steve.

"It runs in the family," Grandfather said.

"What do you mean? I'm the sweet, cheerful one in the family," Uncle Fong said indignantly.

Kitten ran off, calling out, "Help, help, thieves, robbers, bandits!"

Steve grabbed Uncle Fong's wrist. "We'd better leave, or we'll get into real trouble."

They heard a gong sound somewhere among the trees. A man started to shout, "Alarm, alarm!"

"There'll be a mob coming soon," Grandfather said.

"But it's my clan," Uncle Fong protested.

"They won't know you. You've grown old," Grandfather warned.

Steve tugged at Uncle Fong. "They'll just beat you."

Uncle Fong sighed and then turned in a slow circle, looking at everything. "I want to remember it just as it is," he murmured.

Suddenly an object whistled by his ear.

Men, women, and children came out from the trees. They held sticks and brooms and hoes. They waved them over their heads menacingly.

Kitten led them. Her duck waddled angrily at her heels.

In one hand she held a basket. "Thieves, robbers!" she shouted angrily. Then she took something from the basket and threw it.

"Ow." Uncle Fong jumped when it hit him.

The missile rolled near Steve's feet. He picked it up. "It looks like a meat dumpling, but it feels like a rock."

Kitten pelted Uncle Fong with more dumplings.

Finally Uncle Fong turned and raced past them. "It must be one of her cooking mistakes. She was the worst cook in four districts."

Grandfather yelled to Steve, "Run, boy. She's got enough dumplings to knock out an elephant."

The Radio

Ahead of them, they saw, Grandfather's window hung in the air.

"I'll help you through the window," Steve said. He made a cup with his hands.

"No, you first, boy!" Picking Steve up by the waist, Grandfather threw him through the window onto the bed.

As Steve bounced off the mattress, Grandfather tumbled after him. Uncle Fong was the last one through.

With a groan Uncle Fong rolled off the bed and stood up. "So much for sentiment," he grumbled.

Grandfather complained as he got up finally. "My bruises have bruises. They should have named her Tiger, not Kitten."

"Stupid paintbrush," Uncle Fong said as he sat on his bed. He looked ready to cry.

"Here's a souvenir from Dragon Back." Grandfather held up a peach pit between his index finger and thumb. Getting down on his knees, he felt underneath his bed until he came up with a small tin. Then he deposited the peach pit safely in the tin and gave it to Uncle Fong. "Plant this someday and have your own peaches."

Uncle Fong cradled the tin. "Thank you, friend."

Grandfather nudged Steve. "It's your turn to make a wish."

Steve had been thinking about this. He had been growing excited since the idea had first come to him. His heart was pounding now. "I'd like to see my parents again."

Grandfather looked as if he were suddenly in pain. "They've passed on, boy."

Normally Steve would not have risked making Grandfather angry, but the brush had given him new courage. "So had Uncle Fong's sister Kitten. But we saw her. Don't you miss them?"

Grandfather squirmed uncomfortably. "Of course. But you've seen how quirky the paintbrush is. Who knows what will happen?"

Steve couldn't bear to give up now. "But I already have so much trouble remembering them. I try and I try, but I can't see their faces. It's like . . . it's like losing them all over again."

Grandfather looked thoughtful. Then he said softly, "True."

"Then how are you going to paint them?" asked Uncle Fong.

Getting on his knees, Grandfather slid his suitcase out from under the bed again. Steve sniffed the wonderful, mysterious scents as Grandfather opened the lid. Grandfather rummaged around for a little bit. Then he took out a small packet. It was wrapped in red silk.

Reverently he removed the wrapping and held up a black-and-white photo. It seemed to be of someone's living room. On a table sat a big, old-fashioned radio. In front of it a man and woman stood together. The man was in a tuxedo, and the woman was in a fluffy gown. They were holding hands as if they were about to dance. They were so young, they didn't look like his parents.

Steve studied it carefully, trying to memorize their faces. Then he began to paint on a sheet of paper.

Grandfather swallowed. "I shouldn't let you do this. You're just building up your hopes for nothing. And you're going to feel even more hurt than before." However, Grandfather just sat and watched.

So Steve went on painting. He worked quickly, afraid his grandfather would stop him. Many times he looked at the photograph. His hand almost shook with excitement. He concentrated as hard as he could. He wanted to make the magic happen.

When he was done, he put the brush down and studied his work.

"It looks just like them," Grandfather said.

"Do you really think so?" Steve said.

Grandfather studied Steve's eager face. He nodded.

But this time there was no tingle to the picture. Steve rubbed his fingers back and forth over the paper. There still was no spark.

"It didn't work," he said sadly.

"See? There's only so much the paintbrush can do." Grandfather sighed.

Between his fingers Steve felt the paintbrush expand and contract. He thought it was trying to say it was sorry. "It has a personality like a real person," he said.

"A very funny person," Uncle Fong grunted. "One who likes to play mean tricks."

"You were right," Steve said to his grandfather. He wrapped his arms around himself and rocked back and forth. "It's bad to hope, because it just hurts when you fail."

Tears stung the corners of his eyes. He swiped them with the back of his hand.

"Next time listen to me," Grandfather said. He wiped at his eyes. "Must have gotten something in my eyes," he muttered. However, Steve thought Grandfather must have been feeling just as bad as he did.

He stared. "You don't hate my parents?"

Grandfather kept wiping at his eyes. "What made you think that?"

Steve was afraid that he had gone too far. "Because you always get so mad when I talk about them," he said, frightened.

Grandfather gave a snuffle. "What do you expect? If you kick me, of course I'm going to lose my temper. It's the same thing when you try to make me recall them. Why do you keep doing that all the time? Doesn't it hurt you, too?"

"Sure," Steve said, "but as long as I remember them, they're still alive in a way."

Grandfather was silent for a while before he finally scratched his cheek. "I never thought about it that way."

Uncle Fong jerked his head at Grandfather. "You and me, we're two tough old clams who don't like to talk about things. But the boy grew up different."

Grandfather drew his eyebrows together as he studied Steve. Finally he took a deep breath and let it out. "I guess you did. So you have to mourn in your own way. All right. When you need to, ask me about them."

Now that Steve had permission, he suddenly felt very shy. Instead, he tapped the old radio in the photograph. "What a funny old radio."

"It worked better than any of the new ones," Grandfather said.

"I loved that old radio." Uncle Fong sighed.

"What happened to it?" Steve asked.

Grandfather looked away. "I kept that piece of junk too long."

Uncle Fong frowned at Grandfather. "You owe the boy the truth." He turned to Steve. "Your grandfather sold it to a collector. It paid for your parents' funeral."

Steve felt as if someone had punched him in the stomach. "I'm sorry for being so much trouble."

Grandfather drew himself up proudly. "You do what you have to do for family. So why talk about it?"

Steve thought of how Grandfather had made sure he was first through the window. He'd been wrong. His grandfather really did care. He just didn't talk about it. He showed it by his actions. Somehow Grandfather didn't seem so strange anymore.

Steve touched his grandfather's arm. "Thank you." Steve licked his lips and added, "But there's a lot I still don't understand about Chinatown. Sometimes it would help if you would explain things to me."

His grandfather nodded slowly. "Chinatowners are made, not born."

Satisfied, Steve looked back at the photograph. He touched the handsome young man and the pretty young woman. "They wore those clothes when they danced to rock and roll music?"

"No." Grandfather laughed. "They didn't like the music their friends did. They were ballroom dancers."

"I saw them dance once." Uncle Fong tapped his feet on the floor. "They could have turned professional."

Steve bent over the photo, studying the radio in the background. "What kind of music did they like?"

"American ballroom music, like in the old days," Grandfather said.

"Like when we were young," Uncle Fong said. "Your parents had excellent taste."

Steve squinted harder at the photo. He tried to remember every detail about the radio. Then he began to paint on a sheet of paper. Maybe if he gave it back to his grandfather, he wouldn't feel so sad.

Steve was a little anxious when he had finished. Would the magic work this time? Then he felt the tingle pass through his fingertips. And the radio sat on his bed.

Steve was surprised. "Why did the paintbrush work this time?"

Grandfather rubbed his chin. "Maybe the paintbrush only gives you what it can."

Uncle Fong sighed. "So Dragon Back is gone for good."

"Fool," Grandfather said, tapping his head, "it's still here."

Uncle Fong nodded slowly. "I guess it's better to go back there in my memories than in person."

"You can talk to me about Dragon Back whenever you want," Steve said.

Uncle Fong smiled. "All the good times."

"And we'll do the same with your parents, boy," Grandfather promised. He caressed the radio lightly. "You know, your father used to play this night and day."

Steve plugged it into the outlet by the hot plate and turned it on. A waltz began to play.

"Ah," Grandfather sighed. "That was their favorite tune." He set the photograph where they could see it.

The waltz was as gentle and sweet as a breeze on a hot day. Steve closed his eyes, imagining his father and mother floating across a dance floor.

The next song was a lively number. Grandfather said it was a rumba.

Uncle Fong pointed at the radio. "I remember them dancing to that."

The radio played another half dozen songs. Steve's parents had loved all of them. He set the radio on his lap. He felt the music vibrate in his bones. As he felt his parents' music fill him, he didn't feel so lonely anymore.

Uncle Fong rubbed his chin. "That's funny. There's no commercials on this station." He tried to turn the dial. The station never changed. "And you can only get one station."

Steve hugged the radio. "Can I leave it on tonight? I'll keep it low."

Grandfather looked uncertainly at Uncle Fong. Uncle Fong nodded his head sympathetically.

"It will beat his snoring," Uncle Fong said, jerking a thumb at Grandfather.

They set the radio on the table and turned it low. Then Steve painted some brushes for school. "The magic brush stays home," he said.

They carefully placed it back in Grandfather's

suitcase and got ready for bed. Then Grandfather turned off the room light and lowered the new shutter over the new window. The radio dial still shone in the darkness. It cast a soft glow on the ceiling. As Steve listened to the soft music, he thought he saw shadows of dancers above him. The man and woman whirled round and round as he slowly fell asleep.

The Lady on the Moon

The next night as the radio played softly, Steve asked Grandfather and Uncle Fong, "What shall we do tonight?"

Uncle Fong nodded to the window. "Whatever we decide, you can paint over Dragon Back."

Steve was surprised. "Don't you want to try to go there again sometime?"

Uncle Fong shook his head. "I've been thinking over what the old man said, and he's right. I haven't really lost Dragon Back." He tapped his head. "I've got Dragon Back in here." And he touched his heart. "And in here. That's enough."

"Are you sure?" Grandfather asked gently.

Uncle Fong took a deep breath and then slapped his

knees. "Quite sure. We should be looking forward, not backward."

"But what should I paint?" Steve wondered.

Grandfather rubbed the back of his neck sheepishly. "I've thought and thought about it all day over the soap-suds. But no, you'll just make fun of me."

"It couldn't be any worse than Uncle Fong's," Steve said. "His wish got us chased by a duck."

"It was a very vicious duck," Uncle Fong pointed out.

"Please, Grandfather. We won't laugh," Steve said. "Right?" He looked at Uncle Fong.

Uncle Fong folded his arms. "I guess."

Grandfather clasped his hands upon his lap. "I don't think the paintbrush wants us to go back into the past. So let's try legends. Will you paint me the moon?" He glanced around, waiting for them to tease him.

"Why would you want to go there? There's no life on the moon. The scientists all say so." Uncle Fong began to hop from one leg to the other. "We would need space helmets and space suits."

Steve defended his grandfather. "We'll go wherever Grandfather wants."

Grandfather squeezed Steve's arm gratefully. "I don't want the moon of the newspapers and television. I want to go to the moon the way it's supposed to be. I want Chinatown's moon."

"What moon is that?" Steve asked, puzzled.

"A moon like in the stories they tell in Chinatown," Grandfather explained.

Steve shook his head. "Mom and Dad never told me those stories."

Uncle Fong grunted in disgust. "Kids. They turn their backs on everything."

Grandfather held up a hand. "Easy, Fong." And then he said to Steve, "What Chinese stories did they tell you?"

Steve squirmed. "Well, nothing really." He tried to defend them. "But they were pretty busy."

"Yes, of course." Grandfather placed his hands on his knees while he studied Steve. "Chinatown must seem very strange if you don't know the stories."

Steve wriggled uncomfortably. "Sort of."

"Then we'll make you a Chinatowner," Grandfather said. "First we'll begin with Chinatown's moon." He rose from the bed and shaped a tree with his hands and arms. "Here is the beautiful cassia tree. Its leaves are always green. Its flowers are always in bloom. And its bark is so fragrant—it's cinnamon, you know. The tree can never be cut down. In its shade sits the rabbit. He has a mortar and a pestle to grind things. With them he makes magical pills. Eat one, and you live forever." He described to Steve what a mortar and pestle looked like.

"I always thought it was a mean joke to play on the

Lady on the Moon," Uncle Fong said.

"Who is she?" Steve asked.

"She was the wife of a mighty archer," Grandfather explained. "As a reward for his great feats, Heaven sent him pills of immortality. But his wife swallowed them instead. As punishment Heaven exiled her to the moon."

"Where the rabbit keeps her company," Uncle Fong said. He knocked his hand rhythmically against the wall. "So that's all she hears day and night: the rabbit making pills with a mortar and pestle."

"She would listen from her palace," Grandfather said, and waved a hand. "It would be not too close and not too far from the tree."

As Grandfather described the moon, Steve thought he could almost see it. Excitedly he began to paint over the old picture. Within the window he put the cassia tree and the rabbit and the palace. Its roof slanted steeply, like green-tiled mountains. Creatures stood watch on the roof against fires and lightning and other dangers. A porch led to the main door of the palace, which was perfectly round, like a moon gate.

"Nice," Uncle Fong nodded approvingly. "Just like the old stories."

Steve cleaned his brush. "And what does the Lady on the Moon look like?" Steve asked.

"I always thought she would look a little like your grandmother," Grandfather said.

"I never met her," Steve said.

"And I have no pictures," Grandfather said. "But she was beautiful." And in a deep, pleasant voice, he began to sing about the Lady on the Moon.

Steve went to the radio and snapped it off. He listened to his grandfather for a moment. Finally he began to paint the rabbit's mortar and pestle while his grandfather sang.

Steve had no sooner painted the tools when the rabbit grabbed the pestle and began pounding it into the mortar in time to Grandfather's tune.

Suddenly a silvery light poured from the palace's doorway. The light flooded into their room. Steve felt himself carried along its warm, invisible currents. Still singing, Grandfather looked as if he were floating on a river. Kicking like he was swimming, and waving happily, Uncle Fong was swept into the picture too.

Inside, they landed among giant flowers. They were twice as big as anything on Earth. Some chrysanthemums were as big as cabbages.

Grandfather brushed himself off. "The air's so still here."

"You're lucky there is air," Uncle Fong said.

Grandfather plucked a flower from a bush. "Stop thinking. Just enjoy it."

"Maybe you should ask permission before you pick the flowers," Steve suggested.

"But these all belong to the Lady on the Moon—the most beautiful creature in all the heavens. How dare I speak to her?" Grandfather asked.

Soon he had a handful of flowers. He sniffed them appreciatively. "Ah."

In the distance, over the sound of the pestle pounding in the mortar, they heard another sound. It was a soft hiss-hiss-hiss.

Uncle Fong grabbed Grandfather. "It's a snake. I hate snakes."

Grandfather pushed him away. "There aren't any snakes on the moon."

Suddenly the Lady on the Moon appeared in the doorway. Steve and Grandfather bowed, but Uncle Fong just stood there, staring with his mouth open.

"Mind your manners," Grandfather said, and pinched him.

"Ow." Hastily Uncle Fong lowered his head.

The lady bowed back. Then she moved across the porch toward them. Her long gown trailed behind her, making the hissing noises. The silk whispered as it brushed the wooden floor.

Shading his eyes, Steve asked eagerly, "Does she look like Grandmom?"

When Grandfather smiled, he looked years younger. "Yes."

She smiled sweetly. "I seldom have company."

Grandfather drew himself up. "We seldom go out visiting."

He was just about to present the flowers to her when they heard someone shout, "Hey, who ruined my wall?"

Mighty Mister Pang

"I think you have visitors yourself," the Lady on the Moon said. Whirling around, she disappeared into the palace and slammed the door.

Steve felt as if a giant hand had caught him and pulled him back. The next moment he and his grandfather and Uncle Fong were sitting on the floor of their room.

A small man stood in the middle bouncing up and down on his heels. The cigar dropped from the man's mouth. "How did you step out of the wall?" he demanded.

"We have a magic paintbrush," said Steve. "But who are you? How did you get in here?"

Grandfather shushed Steve. "This is Mr. Pang. He owns this place."

"It's a good thing I showed up today to check on my property." Mr. Pang rubbed his chin. "But what's this about a magic paintbrush?"

"Nothing," Steve said quickly. The landlord looked very sly. He pretended to grow angry as he pointed to the painting. "How dare you wreck my nice clean wall!"

That made Steve mad. "The wall hasn't been painted in years. And what about the burned-out lightbulbs? What about the trash? You should take care of those things first."

Mr. Pang folded his arms sternly. "You vandals can't get away with this outrage. There are laws against this. I'll have all of you arrested and thrown in jail."

"You can't do that to them," Steve said bravely. "I'm the one who painted it."

The landlord rubbed his chin with his big, fat thumb. "Well, I'd be willing to forget what you did if . . ."

Grandfather glared at him. "If what?"

"If you give me the paintbrush," the landlord said.

"Grandfather got this from his grandfather," Steve objected.

"It's yours now, Steve," Grandfather said.

"I'm calling the cops," the landlord threatened. "Where's the phone?"

Steve didn't want to give up the brush, but he loved his grandfather more. "Don't harm my grandfather," he said, and he held out the brush.

Mr. Pang grasped it greedily. "So I just paint something on the wall?"

"Yes," Steve said, "but—"

"I want gold and jade and pearls," Mr. Pang said. He was almost drooling. "No, no, wait. Why stop there? I'll need something to put them in. There are thieves all around." He glanced around and headed for the nearest bare patch of wall.

Steve followed him. "We should warn you—"

"So what do I do? Paint like this?" Mr. Pang began splashing paint crudely on the wall. "I always wanted a house big as the Fairmont Hotel," he said. "With red rugs thick as a pig, and huge chandeliers overhead. Something plush, you know? And classy. And all the plates and cups are real gold. And we never have the same ones twice. Just use them once and throw them away."

Mr. Pang's eyes were big and wide, and he kept chattering excitedly. Hastily he painted a mansion big as the Fairmont. The red columns were covered with carved animals painted gold.

All around the mansion he painted fountains and bridges and moon gates. Even when he had covered every square inch with lavish decorations, Mr. Pang wasn't satisfied.

"But I also wanted a banquet with a thousand fancy courses. I should have painted a bigger picture," he whined.

Grandfather sniffed at the open gates. "I think your banquet is inside. I can smell mushrooms frying."

Mr. Pang sniffed at the delightful smell. "Can I paint, or can I paint?" he declared proudly. "Now what do I do?"

"You step through it," Grandfather said.

Mr. Pang eyed the painting. "You don't hit the wall instead?"

"You saw us come out of it," Grandfather said.

As Mr. Pang continued to stare at the painting, Steve finally had a chance to warn him. "Your picture's very nice," he said. Actually, it wasn't, but Steve was too polite to say so. "But sometimes the brush can play tricks on you."

"So what?" As the brush dripped paint onto the floor, Mr. Pang examined his painting cautiously. Suddenly he held the brush like a sword and jabbed Steve. "You go first."

The Life of Luxury

"It's your painting," Steve argued.

"That's right. So any gold or jewels are mine," the landlord warned him.

Grandfather pulled Steve to the side. "I'll go first."

"Why?" Steve asked in surprise.

Grandfather looked hurt. "Do you really have to ask?"

"But I thought you didn't want me," Steve said.

"Where did you get that idea from?"

"Well, you're always scolding me, for one thing," Steve said.

"That was the way we were brought up," Uncle Fong explained. "There was an old saying back in China: Praise the child, spoil the child. Your grandfather was the happiest man in Chinatown when you were born."

"That's enough lovey-dovey," Mr. Pang said. "You can both go."

"All right, all right." Grandfather plunged through the window before Steve.

He really does love me, Steve thought as he followed him.

Uncle Fong came next. "Quit pushing, Pang," he said.

As they stood outside the mansion, a scandalized voice asked, "Sirs, what are you doing dressed like that?"

Steve saw a tall servant running toward them. His hair and eyebrows were blue. Behind him came a dozen servants. They also had blue hair and all wore satin jackets and pants embroidered with unicorns. In their hands they held fancy silk robes on which unicorns were also sewn.

Grandfather bowed politely. "We're just passing through," he said.

Uncle Fong turned in the direction of the window and said, "Pang, come on in. It's safe. Hey!"

"Sirs, you can't be seen in those rags," said Mr. Blue. At his signal the other servants pounced upon Grandfather and Uncle Fong and put unicorn robes on them right over their clothes.

The robes looked like they fit, but Grandfather complained, "This collar's too tight."

"Mine too." Uncle Fong tried to unbutton his collar.

"Sirs, important men must look important,"

Mr. Blue scolded. "These are all the latest fashion." Gently but firmly he shoved Uncle Fong's hands away from the collar.

Mr. Pang stepped through the painting with the brush still in his hand. "Wait a moment. I'm the boss," he shouted. "Why are you dressing those bums in my clothes?"

The puzzled servants whispered among themselves, and then Mr. Blue turned to Grandfather and Uncle Fong. "Sirs, if you don't mind, there's been a terrible mistake."

Grandfather beat Uncle Fong at taking off his robe. "It's quite all right."

"No, take mine," Uncle Fong complained.

"I'll take both," the greedy Mr. Pang said.

The next moment the servants had dressed Mr. Pang in the robes, one over the other. They shrank magically to fit him.

"Now let's eat," said Mr. Pang. He strutted like a peacock toward the mansion.

"Sir, what are you doing?" Mr. Blue demanded in shock. At his signal two dozen hands lifted Mr. Pang high in the air.

Mr. Pang kicked his legs and flailed his arms. He looked like a beetle on its back. "Hey, hey, put me down," he ordered.

"Sir, what would the neighbors think if they saw you walking?" Mr. Blue explained.

And the servants swept Mr. Pang over to a carrying chair. It was decorated with real gold and pearls. Next the servants slid jade-encrusted poles along the sides so the chair could be carried.

Mr. Blue shuddered. "Your feet should never touch dirt, sir."

Crouching beneath the chair poles, they lifted it onto their shoulders. Mr. Pang waved to Grandfather and Steve from behind a curtain on the side of the chair. "This is the life!"

As the servants carried Mr. Pang through the garden, Grandfather nudged Steve. "Let's follow and see what happens."

The servants carried Mr. Pang over bridges and through moon gates, underneath flowering trees and past fragrant beds of flowers.

They bore Mr. Pang through the doors of the mansion and right into a banquet room. The ceiling was so high, Steve could barely see the roof beams. Everything was decorated with gold and jade and pearls.

The servants carried Mr. Pang toward a huge table. It was groaning with golden plates and bowls. On them were fish and roast pigs and ducks. There were also a lot of dishes Steve didn't recognize.

"What's that?" he asked Grandfather, and pointed at a flat, pink something.

"I think it's pickled jellyfish," Grandfather whispered back.

"Ugh," Steve said.

"It's very tasty," Grandfather said. "A real China-towner is always willing to try a dish once."

Steve might try a nibble, but that would be the only time.

Mr. Pang sat down in a teak chair as big as a throne. It was carved like a dragon with silver claws. "I don't know where to begin," he said, smacking his lips.

"Sir." Mr. Blue frowned. "You can't look all messy like a common laborer. You must clean up."

And the other servants brought a large porcelain jar showing the many mansions and palaces in the sky. From the jar they poured water into a huge bowl decorated with the gardens of the sea.

"Yes, of course, I knew that." Mr. Pang laughed nervously. He handed the brush to Mr. Blue and allowed the other servants to wash him.

Steve, Grandfather, and Uncle Fong watched from the doorway. Mr. Blue brought the brush over to Steve and bowed. "Little sir, I believe this really belongs to you."

Steve noticed that the brush hairs matched the color of the servant's hair.

Steve hesitated. "I'm not sure I want it back. The brush plays tricks. You can't trust it," he said.

Mr. Blue smiled politely. "Little sir, magic cannot be tamed. Magic is like Nature. Can you control the rain? And do you blame it when it gets you wet and you catch cold? And yet does that same rain help your crops to grow and feed you?"

Grandfather looked thoughtful. "So we have to learn how to adjust to the magic. We have to survive the bad parts and enjoy the good."

Mr. Blue blinked his blue eyelashes. "I believe that's what I said, sir."

"But how much magic is left in the paintbrush?" Steve asked.

Mr. Blue chuckled. "How much rain is left in the sky, little sir?"

"I hate riddles," Uncle Fong groaned.

"The magic depends on you," Mr. Blue said, and glanced at Uncle Fong. "It depends on what you wish and how hard you wish."

"But I really wanted to see my parents," Steve said.

"You didn't let me finish," Mr. Blue said. "Wishing is only part of it, though. Magic is like riding the unicorn. Some of the time it will take you where it wants to go rather than where you want to."

Uncle Fong remembered his wish. "That seems like most of the time."

Mr. Blue faced Steve. "And, of course, you might outgrow the magic one day."

"I never will," Steve promised. Taking the brush, he hid it inside his sleeve and felt the hairs tickle him in greeting.

"We will see, little sir," Mr. Blue said. "Now if you'll excuse me, I have the master to serve." And with a polite bow, he returned to Mr. Pang's side.

As he wiped his hands on a silk towel, Mr. Pang smacked his lips. "Boy, oh, boy, am I hungry." He did not notice that he no longer had the paintbrush. "I'd like the beef with mushrooms. It's made me hungry just smelling it."

Mr. Blue shook his head. "Sir, you must have smelled our meal. That dish is only for common folk like us. You deserve far better fare." He clapped his hands.

From the kitchen marched a servant. In his hands was a silver tray. On the tray was a gold dish, and on the dish were things that looked like black chips. "The Twelve Friendly Funguses," Mr. Blue announced.

Mr. Pang pushed the dish aside. "Take it away! What else is there to eat?"

The servant looked disappointed as he removed the dish. He returned with a new dish.

"Snail Tails," declared Mr. Blue proudly.

"That's more like it." Mr. Pang eagerly picked up a pair of chopsticks.

"Sir!" Mr. Blue cried out, scandalized. He pried the chopsticks out of Mr. Pang's hand. "Please, allow me." Holding the chopsticks, he selected a tasty morsel and dangled it in front of Mr. Pang.

Mr. Pang opened his mouth like a baby bird, and Mr. Blue guided the Snail Tail carefully inside his mouth. A second servant cleaned Mr. Pang's mouth. A third put a hand on his jaw.

"Chew a hundred times, sir, to savor the flavor," Mr. Blue instructed.

Mr. Pang frowned and tried to pull free, but two more servants gripped him. As Mr. Pang began to chew, Mr. Blue kept count.

When he had chewed one hundred times, a sixth servant patted Mr. Pang on the back.

"Now please burp for us, sir," Mr. Blue requested politely.

Mr. Pang pounded the table. "This is ridiculous," he said, rising angrily. "I haven't lived sixty years to be treated like an infant."

When he tried to leave, the servants seized him and shoved him back into his chair.

Mr. Blue raised his hands in shock. "Sir, you haven't finished. You must eat the entire banquet."

Mr. Pang's eyes bulged. "Finish everything? And when is that?"

"When you've eaten all one thousand dishes," Mr. Blue informed him.

"I'll eat what I want, and I'll eat when I want," Mr. Pang shouted. He tried to get up again, but the servants held him down.

Another servant took the empty dish into the

kitchen and returned with a new one.

"Hump Stump of Camel," the servant cried happily.

"And don't forget, master," Mr. Blue reminded Mr. Pang. "Chew each bite one hundred times."

"But that will take forever," Mr. Pang wailed.

It was a mistake to keep his mouth open that long. A servant took the opportunity to shove a biteful of camel hump between Mr. Pang's lips.

Mr. Pang whipped his head from side to side. Then he tried to spit it out, but a servant clapped a hand over his mouth. "Chew, sir."

"And don't worry, sir. We have plenty of camel hump," Mr. Blue promised.

Mr. Pang tried to protest, but every time he opened his mouth, he was fed more camel hump. When he tried to get away, two servants pinned him to the chair.

Steve studied the next dish that a servant had brought. It looked like yellow-and-purple mush.

Steve started to feel sorry for the landlord. "Do you think we should help Mr. Pang?" he asked his grand-father and Uncle Fong.

Uncle Fong stopped him. "No, I think he's got more help than he wants right now."

Grandfather nodded. "But let's visit him later. Maybe he'll be more reasonable about things."

Steve grinned. Uncle Fong and Grandfather were much smarter than Steve had thought at first. "I guess we shouldn't interrupt his supper."

Laughing, they left the mansion and stepped out of the painting. And when they were back in their room, Steve painted shutters so they could shut out Mr. Pang's mansion.

The Rescue

That day they heard from the other tenants that Mr. Pang's family had come looking for him. Of course, they couldn't find any sign of him.

The next night Steve examined the paintbrush. "I wonder how much we should trust the brush. The servant said it could be pretty quirky."

"Well, the Lady on the Moon was pretty good," Grandfather said, "until Mr. Pang interrupted it."

"Still, we don't know how it would have turned out," Uncle Fong said.

Grandfather glanced back and forth between the Moon Lady's window and Mr. Pang's window. "Maybe because some wishes are good ones and some are bad."

"What's so wrong with wanting to go home?" Uncle Fong demanded.

"Perhaps the paintbrush was trying to tell you that you can't ask for certain things," Grandfather suggested.

Uncle Fong scowled at him. "Paintbrushes aren't philosophers."

"But this came from my grandfather, and he was a kind of philosopher," Grandfather explained. "As a young man he had gone to a monastery to study a type of Buddhism called Ch'an. I think the Japanese call it Zen."

He gazed at the paintbrush. "My grandfather told me to pray that I would see a unicorn, because unicorns bring joy to the heart. I wonder if that applies to hairs from a unicorn's tail."

"What was joyful about returning to Dragon Back?" Uncle Fong demanded. "I've still got bumps from my sister's dumplings."

"You did enjoy parts of your trip," Steve said.

"And going there made you realize it's not what you really wanted," Grandfather pointed out.

"Help, help," they heard a faint voice.

Steve felt guilty. "That must be Mr. Pang. I'm surprised his family didn't hear him."

Uncle Fong shrugged. "Since they couldn't see him, they probably thought it was someone's radio in the distance."

"I guess we should do something," Grandfather said to Uncle Fong.

"I'll help you," Steve said, feeling relieved.

To their surprise even Uncle Fong agreed to help. "I'd better go along this time, too. Who knows what new tricks that paintbrush has in store for you?"

"You're getting soft, old man," Grandfather teased.

Uncle Fong drew himself up huffily. "It's nothing of the kind. I just don't want to have to break in a new pair of roommates. It's been hard enough with you two."

Uncle Fong didn't fool Steve anymore. "You're just like a crab. You're all hard on the outside, but you're mushy on the inside."

Uncle Fong tried to scowl, but his mouth turned up in a grin. "Nothing good is going to come from spoiling you this way. So don't blame me when you grow up rotten."

"I won't," Steve promised, and opened the shutters.

"Sometimes I forget what a good friend you can be," Grandfather said affectionately.

Uncle Fong waved his hand. "Enough already. Let's go." But when he thought they weren't looking, he wiped his eyes. Uncle Fong was as good as a real uncle.

Grandfather leaned his head toward the window. Then he cupped his hand behind his ear. "We should find out what's going on inside first. Maybe I can over-hear something."

"We can do better than that," Steve said. Getting out the paintbrush, he carefully painted a small window on the mansion. "Now we can peek inside at Mr. Pang."

Uncle Fong insisted on looking first. He started to giggle. "It serves the pig right."

Grandfather was next. He laughed too. "I heard the servant. Pang's only up to five hundred and three."

When Steve looked through the window, he saw Mr. Pang. He was so huge that he filled his chair. His fancy robes had split at the seams. And his eyes bulged like Ping-Pong balls.

"Please. No more. No more. Or I'll burst," he begged. His arms were tied to the chair with golden cords. He waved his fingers feebly. The banquet table was littered with empty bowls and plates.

The servants ignored him. They brought a golden platter. On it were a dozen odd-colored eggs. "Sir, here is five hundred and four: Hermit's Fungus over Peacock Feet. And remember: a hundred chews per bite."

"No, my jaws are worn out," Mr. Pang said, and clamped his mouth shut. However, one servant pried his jaws open while a second fed him.

"He looks like a balloon with little strings for arms and legs," Steve said. He felt a little guilty for leaving Mr. Pang there so long.

"But how do we get him away from his servants?" Grandfather wondered.

"I think I know how," Steve said. Quickly he painted a small, ugly black cloud. Lightning bolts bristled from the side like porcupine quills. Sheets of rain fell from it.

Leaning forward, he gently blew it right through

the tiny window he had just painted and into the mansion. Thunder rumbled and lightning flashed. They heard the servants shout frantically from inside, "Help! It's flooding in here!"

Uncle Fong patted Steve's shoulder. "How'd you get so smart? You couldn't have gotten it from your grandfather. It must be from your grandmother."

The three climbed through the window and ran into the garden. Streams of water poured out of the mansion. They struggled up the steps through the torrent.

Uncle Fong pulled his collar up. "Maybe you should have painted a smaller cloud," he said.

When Steve splashed through the doorway, he had to agree. Inside, the mansion was a mess. The cloud floated beneath the roof raining water below. Lightning flashed like bulbs on a camera. Then thunder boomed. He thought he was inside a huge bass drum.

On the walls away from the rain, fires burned. "Oh, no. Lightning must have started fires," Grandfather said.

The water was up to Mr. Pang's knees. He struggled to get up, but the cords held him to the massive chair. "Please help me," he called.

"Will you try to take my paintbrush ever again?" Steve asked.

Mr. Pang shuddered. "No, never. I don't want to ever see any brush ever. Not toothbrushes. Not hair brushes. Not shoe brushes. Nothing with any kind of brush."

Steve folded his arms. "And will you fix up the apartment building?" he asked.

Mr. Pang wiggled up and down on the chair seat. "Yes, yes. I'll make it nice as the Fairmont Hotel," he said desperately.

So Uncle Fong picked up a porcelain cup and broke it on the table. With the pieces they sawed at the cords. When they fell away, though, Mr. Pang could not stand up.

Grandfather scratched his head. "I don't think he can move fast enough to escape his servants."

Steve saw the carrying chair and pointed at it. "We can use that," he said.

Quickly they brought the chair over. However, Mr. Pang was so huge that he barely fit.

The three of them strained to lift the chair off the floor. "Maybe we should have saved him after only three hundred dishes. Now he's too heavy," Uncle Fong said, panting.

"No, no, don't leave me here," Mr. Pang moaned.

Slowly they waded through the water and out into the garden.

They saw the servants in the distance carrying piles of towels. They threw them down when they saw Mr. Pang trying to leave.

"Sir, sir! Come back! Where are you going?" Mr. Blue called.

Mr. Pang beat the sides of the chair. "Faster, faster," he shouted urgently.

"Oof," Uncle Fong puffed. "We're going as fast as we can. You try getting thinner, Fatty."

"Maybe we should just roll him along," Grandfather suggested with a chuckle.

Somehow they staggered to the window. The servants had almost caught up to them now.

Mr. Pang grabbed Grandfather and clung to him for dear life. "Don't let them take me," he wailed.

"Not if we can help it," Grandfather promised.

Steve and Grandfather each took an arm, and Uncle Fong took his legs.

"On three," Grandfather said. "Ready?"

When they nodded their heads, Grandfather counted, "One, two, three."

"Hurry," Mr. Pang said, looking behind them.

Together they heaved the landlord out of the chair. In the same motion they flung him toward the window. Mr. Pang's head and chest popped through, but not his hips.

"My sister's dumplings," Uncle Fong swore. "The pig's stuck."

Mr. Pang kicked his legs frantically. "Don't let them take me back."

"We'll have to shove him," Grandfather said. "On three again. One, two, three."

Together they lunged toward Mr. Pang. Their shoulders hit Mr. Pang at the same time. With a loud popping noise Mr. Pang fell through the window.

He gave a squeal each time someone climbed through the window onto him. When they were on the other side, Steve got a notebook and quickly wrote in it. Then he brought it back to Mr. Pang. "Here's a contract with all your promises. Please sign it," he said, and held out a pen.

Mr. Pang shook his head. All his chins wriggled. "I was under pressure."

Uncle Fong called through the window. "I forgot. Just how many dishes does he have to go?"

Mr. Blue appeared on the other side of the painted window. "The chef is very upset. He says the master will have to start over. Please come back, sir." The servants reached out for Mr. Pang.

Uncle Fong jerked his head at the servants. "So what will it be? Keep your promise, or go back?"

Mr. Pang shivered. "I couldn't eat the lizard gizzards again. Where do I sign?"

Steve held out his notebook. "Right here."

However, Uncle Fong grabbed it instead. "There's one more thing, though." And he scribbled a new promise on the contract.

Mr. Pang raised his head indignantly. "I will not wear a T-shirt that says I'm a greedy pig."

Uncle Fong picked up an ankle. "Enjoy your dinner

then. Steve, give me a hand, will you?"

Mr. Pang glanced at the window. Two dozen hands stretched through the window, ready to take him.

His eyes grew wide with fright. "I'm signing. I'm signing," he said, and wrote out his name.

Dancing on the Moon

The very next day an army of workers came into the apartment building. They replaced the lights. They painted the walls. They carpeted the floors.

The tenants gathered in the hallway to watch. "This is Saturday. Do you know how much it costs to have all these people work today?" a man said, scratching his head.

"What's gotten into Mr. Pang?" a woman wondered.

Uncle Fong chuckled. "Maybe he got more than he wished for."

Grandfather dug his elbow into Uncle Fong from one side, and Steve nudged him from the other.

"Uh . . . or not," Uncle Fong said, rubbing his ribs.

Grandfather folded his arms as he watched all the activity. "Maybe it won't be as nice as the Fairmont

Hotel, but it will be a lot better than it was."

The workers came over with paint cans and brushes and tried to go into their room. Grandfather hurriedly blocked the doorway. "That's all right. You just leave this room to us."

"Mr. Pang gave us special orders to do this room," the head painter protested.

"We'll take care of Mr. Pang," Grandfather said. Putting a hand on the painter's chest, he gently pushed him to the side.

When Uncle Fong and Steve had slipped into the room, Grandfather immediately shut the door. "Where should we go tonight?" he asked.

Uncle Fong stared at the two shuttered windows. "Maybe we should just let the workers cover them up."

Grandfather sighed. "I could do without Mr. Pang's window, but I would miss looking at our Chinatown moon."

"I'd miss the magic," Steve said.

Uncle Fong squirmed and muttered something. "What did you say, old man?" Grandfather demanded.

Uncle Fong shrugged. "I said that I'd miss the dreaming even more than the magic."

"It wasn't even the dreaming. It was the hoping," Grandfather said.

Uncle Fong grunted approvingly. "You're getting smarter the longer you hang around me."

"Maybe you're right. Maybe we'd better go back to

the way things were," Grandfather said.

Steve thought about their days before the paint-brush and felt like crying.

With a weary nod Uncle Fong got up. "I'll get the painters."

At that moment, though, they heard a nervous tap from behind the shutters of Mr. Pang's window. "Sirs, please don't do that."

Uncle Fong went over to the window and spoke through the closed shutters. "We've seen your kind of hospitality. Forget it."

"I understand if you don't want our leftovers," the voice said sadly. "It's not very fancy. It's just our humble fare."

Grandfather came over. "How humble?"

"It's only beef and mushrooms," the voice said.

"Did you say beef?" Before they could stop him, Uncle Fong had thrown open the shutters. On the other side of the window was Mr. Blue. He held a steaming bowl in his hands.

Uncle Fong took it and sniffed. "It smells heavenly," he said, and snatched it from Mr. Blue.

"I have another simple dish, too," Mr. Blue said, and started to bend over to get another bowl.

Grandfather caught Uncle Fong before he could sample his dish. "What's the catch? Is it going to give us pink stripes?" he asked Mr. Blue.

Mr. Blue looked hurt when he straightened. "Sir, we

only want to please you." He held out the second bowl. "Twice-cooked pork, sir?"

Uncle Fong eagerly shouldered Grandfather out of the way. "Now, we can't insult the fellow by refusing," he said, taking the pork dish in his hands.

As Mr. Blue raised a platter of steamed fish, he cleared his throat. "If I may be so bold, the Lady on the Moon has been quite upset. She expected you to visit again long ago."

"She did?" Grandfather asked wistfully.

"I have it on good authority," Mr. Blue replied, handing the platter to Grandfather with a bow. "I'll fetch the dirty dishes tomorrow morning, sir, when I bring you breakfast." And he closed the shutters himself.

At that moment they heard faint drumming from behind the moon window.

Steve got out the paintbrush. He felt the familiar tingle. "I think the paintbrush is trying to tell us that it's sorry."

Grandfather turned and asked them, "Well, what do you think?"

"I have done the safe thing all my life," Uncle Fong said, heading toward the window. "It's time to live a little."

"You hate the paintbrush's tricks. What if you wind up with pink polka dots?" Grandfather asked.

Uncle Fong turned so they could see his profile. "A handsome man looks good even in polka dots," he said.

When Grandfather opened the shutters to the moon window, they saw the Lady upon her porch.

"I have made some rice," she said, indicating a bronze bowl with a lid.

Grandfather cradled the dish. "We have only humble fare, my Lady."

The Lady lifted her head and sniffed the air. "But it smells delicious," she said.

Steve turned on the radio so that they would have soft dinner music. Then he, Grandfather, and Uncle Fong all stepped through the window. Together they dined on the moon. Even the Lady said she had never eaten better.

As Uncle Fong sat back, stuffed, he sighed with contentment. "The world always looks rosier on a full stomach."

The Lady sighed. "Some peaches would be so nice to finish off the meal."

Steve hated to disappoint her. "We know a place where there's some delicious ones. I could paint Dragon Back again."

Uncle Fong rubbed the bumps on his head from his sister's dumplings. "But the peaches are guarded by a she-dragon."

"A pity," the Lady said. "It's been so long since I've had peaches. If I even had a pit, at least I could plant it."

Uncle Fong coughed. "I have a pit."

The Lady smiled. "I would count it a great favor."

"Consider it done," Uncle Fong said gallantly. He climbed back into their room and brought back the little tin. "It will be worth the wait for the tree to grow."

"But the soil on my moon is magical," the Lady said, taking the pit from the tin.

When Uncle Fong had dug a hole, the Lady dropped it in and covered it up.

A green shoot poked up immediately. Uncle Fong sat down with a surprised plop. "Good heavens."

"My moon soil is almost as rich as Dragon Back's," the Lady said with a smile.

They watched as the shoot grew into a sapling, and the sapling into a tree. In a moment the tree's branches were bowing over with ripe peaches.

Trembling, Uncle Fong plucked one. "It's just like home."

Grandfather nudged him. "Ready to start dreaming again?"

Uncle Fong looked ready to cry. "I'm just so out of practice."

The Lady put her hand on his shoulder. "You'll learn."

With a bow, Uncle Fong presented the peach to the Lady. "For you, Lady."

She turned it over in her hands and sniffed it. "It smells delicious." And then she bit it. "And it tastes as good as it smells." She took another bite and laughed as the juice ran down her chin.

Uncle Fong picked peaches for the rest of them, and they were as good as those of Dragon Back.

After they had eaten their fill, the rabbit played a drum. Grandfather sang, and the Lady on the Moon danced.

As she swirled by Steve, she leaned over. "Look up, Steve."

He lifted his head to gaze up. There, in the black sky, their feet skipping over the stars, he thought he saw his mother and father dancing too, dancing just for him.

"They're not gone as long as you remember them," the Lady whispered, and drifted away.

And lying down upon the moon and staring up at the sky, Steve had never felt happier.

The next morning, when Steve woke, he felt his grandfather's arm around him. They were back in their bed. His grandfather and Uncle Fong must have carried him back. At first it had been strange to lie so close to Grandfather, but now Steve liked it.

Their room looked just as tiny and just as cramped as ever, but then he smelled dumplings steaming. He twisted his head to glance at the windows. The scent was coming from behind Mr. Pang's window. The dumplings would make a tasty breakfast.

And he could hear the Lady singing a cheerful tune behind the moon window. He wondered what other stories they could explore. When he went out into Chinatown, he was going to have to keep his eyes and ears open for more stories.

No, he was wrong. The room wasn't small after all. Nor was Chinatown. Grandfather had said: China-towners are made, not born.

Carefully Steve felt for the brush beneath his pillow and felt it tingle in greeting.

Across from them, he heard, Uncle Fong got up with a yawn. "Where do we go tonight, Steve?"

Grandfather sat up. "Let's each think about it today. We want to be careful."

Uncle Fong tapped his temple. "And crafty."

What had Mr. Blue said? Magic cannot be tamed. It was a wild unicorn ride. "And we also have to be ready to laugh," Steve said.

In his hand he felt the paintbrush stir, eager to open new worlds for them.

He couldn't wait either.